I Miss My Teacher!

By Lisa Thompson, M.Ed

Author: Lisa Thompson
Illustrator: A&A Fomin

In March of 2020, teachers and students alike were forced to completely reimagine what "going to school" would look like in the wake of the Covid-19 pandemic. Abruptly and without warning, students were told to gather their essential items and become computer technology pros in a matter of days, in order to reconnect with their teachers and classmates from home. This story, told through the eyes of a 2nd grade child, takes a close and thoughtful look at what was lost in the transition to remote learning. *I Miss My Teacher* is filled with honest feelings and reminiscence from the perspective of the elementary school student. Filled with colorful and poignant illustrations, this book captures the essence and importance of the teacher-student relationship, and can help your child navigate and process their feelings during this challenging time.

First Edition: June 2020
Printed in the United States of America: June 2020
ISBN: 978-1-0878-8826-2

I Miss My Teacher!

This book is dedicated to all the students who have touched my life in a meaningful way. This work of love would not be possible without your gifts, talents and unique personalities. You have shaped my career as a teacher and I LOVE YOU ALL!

-Mrs.Thompson

I miss my teacher.
I miss seeing her every day.
It is not the same as being in school
with all of my friends.

I miss my teacher.
We start our day with mindful meditations.
It helps us to clear our minds and to focus.

I miss my teacher.
My class has flexible seating.
That means we get to sit where we want,
even with our friends!

I miss my teacher.
I miss seeing all the things on the walls of the classroom.

I miss my teacher.
I miss her calling us for carpet time,
where we share ideas from a story we have
been reading.

I miss my teacher.
I miss learning different ways to solve
math problems in my head.
We each think out loud and share how we
solved it to our classmates.
That helps us learn new ways to solve a
problem.

I miss my teacher.
She shows us how to fix problems.
Now we are all problem solvers!

I miss my teacher.
During choice time, we get to decide what
we want to learn more about.
Reading, math, or science?
It's our choice!
I miss that!

I miss my teacher.
She shows us games that make cleaning up more fun!

I miss my teacher.
She takes us through the steps of the writing process.
We need to make sure our writing is third-grade ready!

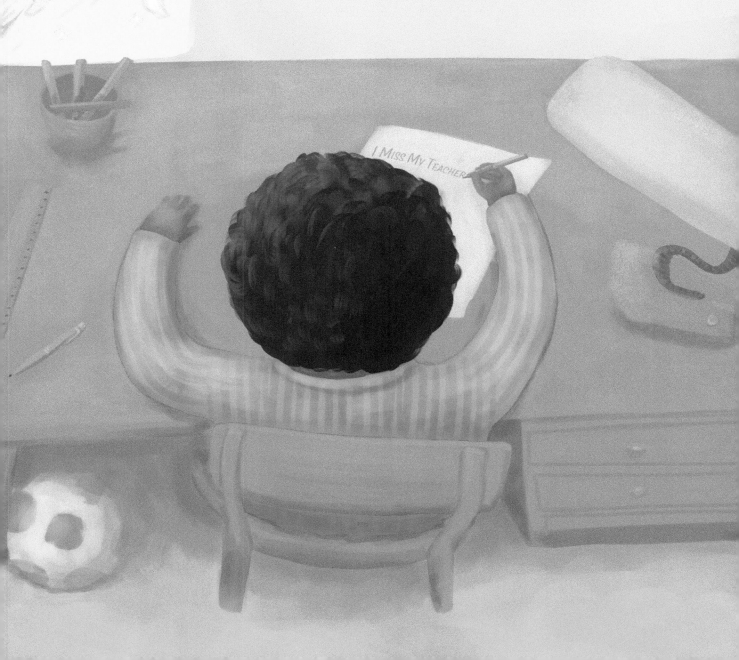

I miss my teacher.
My teacher helps us to come up with creative ways to make connections to our thinking.

I miss my teacher.
She tells us how smart we are and that
everyone has their own gift.
We just have to use it.

I miss my teacher.
My teacher always says,
"Make your own choice.
You don't have to ask me."
I like having the freedom to think on my own.

I miss my teacher.
I love how she takes us out for recess to
run and play. She always says,
"Be safe and be careful."

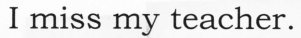

I miss my teacher.
On Tuesdays, I raise my hand to help pass
out the important papers.
My teacher always gives everyone a chance
to help each week.

I miss my teacher.
She has a contest to see who can be the
quietest when we walk to lunch,
music, art and P.E.
We love to play the quiet game.

I miss my teacher.
On Healthy Fridays, we eat lunch in the classroom with the teacher
and our friends.
We show our healthy choices and talk about them with each other.

Some of us bring our lunch.
Some of us buy from the cafeteria.
We try to make the healthiest choices for our brain.

I miss my teacher.
Since we are learning from home, I only get to see her on the computer during our meeting time.
It's not the same as seeing her at school.

I miss my teacher.
Things feel really weird now.
I am learning at home instead of at school
with my teacher and my classmates.

I miss my teacher.
I will be glad when things feel
normal again!

I miss my teacher.
I miss seeing her every day.
I miss my teacher and I know my teacher
misses me too!

For Parents

During this challenging time in our nation's history, you may be faced with uncertainty, anxiety, stress, and some despair. You have been quickly thrown into the role of a teacher on top of your typical job and may be feeling overwhelmed.

Between trying to figure out the "new way of doing math", following a reading program, completing work packets or troubleshooting technology issues, getting your child to sit down and focus for a brief time can be quite challenging when they're at home! My message to you is this:

You were a teacher long before your child stepped into the classroom.

You taught them how to speak, to walk, to eat and how to make sense of the world around them. Please give yourself some grace and know that you are doing the best you can. You are appreciated. Take advantage of this extra closeness to see the good in your new role. Step back, take a walk, play a family game, look at old photos, have an inside picnic. Make joyful memories!

From one teacher to another, when a child knows they are loved, supported, and cared for, they will be successful no matter the outside circumstances.

The Story

When I walked out of the classroom on March 13th, 2020, my ideas and perceptions on the role of "teacher" walked out with me. I thought we would be out for only a couple of weeks. We were told to have the students take home their computer devices, library books, math books and other personal items they might need to work from home.

With extremely limited time and notice, we worked quickly to get the students everything they needed, what we needed, and set off into this "temporary" adventure in remote learning.

The days building up to the transition were total confusion. Administration sent several memos daily, sometimes hourly detailing new instructions with district decisions on how best to take control of the situation at hand. Everyone was feeling anxious and confused, but still trying to maintain a sense of calm and stability for the student's sake.

Over the next few days, a gut feeling was telling me this would indeed become the new normal, and I began to instinctively prepare the classroom by cleaning and organizing materials, books a n d bulletin board displays. I became overwhelmed at the thought that students might not have the support or everything they needed to be successful learners outside of the classroom, so I prepared packets for math, reading, social studies and science for them.

At the end of the last day, as I said my last physical "good- bye" to my students, I couldn't help but hug them as they left to the buses and parent pick-up. I hugged the ones who went to after-care, and the ones who walked with other students to their bus. My heart sank as I watched with tears in my eyes because

I knew... I just knew this would be the last time I saw them in the classroom together as a community of learners.

Soon after, the message came that we would indeed not be returning to school for the remainder of the year and would be moving to a virtual at-home model of learning. As a teacher, this required implementing assignments on a new platform online, navigating parents and technical issues, answering questions, checking emails all while caring for my own family and keeping my sanity in check!

As the weeks went by, a theme started to develop

during our online meetups. My students would tell me they missed me and their friends. They would reminisce about the things we used to do in the classroom as a group. As I listened to their stories, I began to think, why not write a book about our classroom? A way to provide a sense of normalcy and give students something to relate to. I wrote this book through the eyes of a second grader. This is my gift of love to them and all students who really just miss their teacher.

Love,
Lisa Thompson

About the Author

Lisa Thompson, M.Ed has been an educator for 28 years. After receiving her bachelor's in early childhood education, she went on to receive a master's in elementary education. She is an adjunct professor at Tidewater Community College based in Virginia, as well as founder of a one- on-one tutoring program for k-12 students. Outside of leadership in the classroom, she is a published writer and was twice awarded Teacher of the Year by her local school districts. Lisa believes that an environment where reading is valued and seen as a tool both for gaining and reflecting on knowledge can help children become life-long readers.